THE MYSTERY OF THINGS

RANDOM SELECTIONS
FROM A NOVEL

CHARLES CARUSO

49 Morton St. - 7C/212 924 2550/ccarusoc@aol.com

Flashes   2

BARCELONA

Vera bent and kissed her husband on the brow, brushing back a few long white hairs.

He was very old. In his prime he had been one of Spain's most famous actors. On the wall behind his chair were photographs of him with Europe's greatest performers, all costumed opulently, smiling triumphantly in their days of praise.

He spoke to her in Spanish.

Vera, putting on her hat, translated.

"He said, 'Come back soon. Without you I have no life.'"

A nurse straightened a pillow behind his head.

Leading Tom to the door, Vera said, "I'm sorry the interview didn't work out . . . . I suppose it wasn't such a good idea . . . . But he sees so few people these days."

"It was an honor to meet him."

"Sometimes he calls for his mother and father . . . . The other day he said, 'How many more miles to Barcelona? Why is it taking so long? This is a very long trip.' "

*

SUNDAY STROLL

Big doings in town this shiny Sunday.

Two major events: the library's annual book sale and the Red Cross's flower auction on the village green.

"Come on, big guy," Tom Cavanaugh said to his son Danny. "Let's go buy some books." Then in a whisper: "And some flowers for Mommy."

So there they went, down the well-loved, sun-strewn street, seeing familiar faces, people in their Sunday best.

"Isn't he getting big, Tom," and "aren't you looking chipper."

Holding a little hand, Tom Cavanaugh walked abroad.

In the library yard there were rows on rows of books on tables. So many writers, Tom thought. Who would have thought they had so much ink in them? Last year's best-sellers, discarded now. A whole life between battered bindings. Who will buy?

Danny was impatient to get to the flowers. He tugged Tom's sleeve.

"OK, OK, Mamma's boy."

They took the short cut along the narrow stone wall by the brook.

 Danny led. He knew the way.

"*Who will buy this wonderful morning?*" Tom sang, warily following the boy. "*I'm so high . . . .*"

"Be careful, Daddy," Danny said, looking back.

"That's right. Good boy. You take care of me. I could fall."

Then the flower sale. The party-colored blossoms in fragrant wagons by the fountain and monument. And all the smiles.

"These, Daddy."

"Fine. She'll like forsythia all right."

Danny insisted on carrying home the bright sprays. He ran along at Tom's side, the petals shaking, throwing yellow shadows on his eager face.

Passing the May-white cherry tree, they heard church bells.

This is the best of life, Tom thought suddenly. There'll never be anything better.

*

TRESTLE

On their long weekend drives Tom Cavanaugh liked to sing. Anne appreciated the serenading but was reserved in her praise.

"At least you know the words," she said, then kindly added:

"And you carry a tune very well."

He didn't need much more urging.

Once, during their Revolutionary War phase, they were exploring the Hudson, made a turn and saw a hillside bright with white flowers.

"Let's stop," Anne said.

Tom pulled over and they got out and found themselves on a cliff overlooking a deep ravine. The flowering hill was across a sluggish green-coated stream moving far below them. A narrow wooden railroad trestle spanned the stream.

"You couldn't tell from the road it was cut off like this," Tom said.

"They're so beautiful . . . . I think they're hyacinth."

The blossoms foamed down the hill like a waterfall.

"Come, on," Tom said.

"I'm not going out on that rickety thing."

"Come on. You want to see the pretty flowers."

They started across the trestle, carefully stepping on the oil-darkened ties with the turgid green water far below.

"What if there's a train?"

"Nah. This thing hasn't been used in years."

The ties were too close together to take easily one at a time, too far apart for two at a time.

"Hold my hand and don't look down," Tom said.
A wind rose and they stopped, swaying.
"We're half way . . . just a little more . . . . "
Holding hands above the water in the wind, waiting for a whistle, they walked a high walk.

When they were across, Anne plopped around flatfooted, like a child, enjoying the firm earth.

"This is better . . . solid," she said.

Then they climbed through the powerfully scented whiteness. They passed old stone walls and the droppings of small animals. Stopping at a tree, they turned to look back. Stretching far into the distance beyond the trestle, a corn field, dark green in late summer, moved lightly in the wind, gold tassels swaying. They sat on a stone and looked out at the tawny green fields and the blue hills. The sweet scent enveloped them.

the tawny green fields and the blue hills. The sweet scent enveloped them.

"Pretty," Anne said. She drew back a strand of hair with a finger and lifted her chin. There was a tiny heart-shaped birthmark under her left ear.

"You have nice ears," Tom said.

"They stick out."

"No they don't."

She looked up and pouted her mouth. He kissed her and her hand came over.

Then suddenly a freight train clattered fiercely across the trestle.

Tom and Anne looked at each other.

"Jesus Christ," Tom said. "Jesus Christ."

They were quiet for a moment, watching the train's cars bearing the names of faraway states.

Anne said: "Getting back to the car is going to be quite an adventure."

*

SUMMER'S LAST SWIM

Tom Cavanaugh rose from his desk to stretch. He worked out languidly, throwing easy punches at no one in particular. From his window he saw his Andre Hill neighbors working in their gardens.

Anne was out marketing and Claudia was up at the Holmes's backyard pool for one of the summer's last swims.

Then a siren shredded the afternoon calm.

Tom saw an ambulance red-blinking past his window, flashing up the hill.

He dropped his pen and ran through the kitchen to the back door and across the lawn, the sharp grass cutting his bare feet.

Two young mothers were running too, eyes wide.

"It's stopped at the Holmes's!" one of them screamed.

Tom's world plunged crazily as he ran.

"Claudia!" he shouted.

The gaily colored ambulance was halted at the Holmes's.

Then, unaccountably, it started up again and moved off, winking and moaning down the hill into New Jersey.

At the pool the children were splashing happily.

"Daddy, what's wrong?" Claudia cried. "You look strange. Where are your shoes?"

Tom waved and sat down heavily against a tree. His heart banged against his chest.

*

SHIRTS

Tom Cavanaugh stepped out of his house onto Tappan Street. A half-dozen shirts hung from his arm. He was frowning. A garbage truck stood roaring at the curb. We leave the serenity of our homes for the crash and thunder of the city. And shirts to take -- *and* tailor, drugstore, groceries, chores and errands -- the bane of living alone. Plus a railroad train to catch with its iron schedule. Not like the fifteen-minute subway commute to my last job.

Tom set out for the Chinese laundry on Carmine Street. He was uncertain whether to carry his book in the hand that held the shirts or the other. He keep switching uncomfortably. As a result, without his knowledge, one of the sleeves of a shirt fell loose from the bundle and hung down absurdly.

He reached the laundry. A sign in the door said BACK IN 10 MINITS. Christ, Tom aloud. He banged on the door impatiently. Two satin-haired children looked up from their game on the floor, eyes bright with alarm. Oh God, now I've scared his kids. I have to get a newspaper. He walked to the corner. Looking in a store window, Tom noticed the hanging sleeve, pulled it up and cursed his clumsiness, and his loneliness. Did we ever think we'd be alone?

He stood at the candy store counter waiting to pay. A tall, well-tailored women eyed him and his ridiculous shirts. He stared back.

Time-pressed now, Tom was walking quickly, cursing again.

That little jerk, deserting his customers at the start of the morning. Someone ought to wise him up that this ain't Taiwan.

At the laundry again, Tom saw that the offending sign was gone from the door. He opened it roughly.

The laundryman was sitting cross-legged on the floor with his eyes closed.

He was playing a stringed instrument.

*

BOXES

"But don't you see?" Tom Cavanaugh said. "This just proves he wasn't good enough for you . . . . He didn't deserve you."

His daughter Jo was silent, putting things in boxes.

"He wasn't smart enough to appreciate you . . . with all his literary clubs and fancy fraternities."
Jo tried to lift a carton onto the sofa.
"I can get that," Tom said.
"Oh, Daddy," she said with tears in her eyes.
Tom was helping Jo move out of an apartment where she had been living with a young man.
"Remember as a kid you used to say 'gebby' for spaghetti? . . .'Are we gonna have gebby for dinner tonight, Daddy?' "
"I still do," Jo said, sniffling. "It made Chip laugh . . . .Then he'd say it too . . . . He could be very nice."

"I'm sure he could . . . But I think it's best that it ended now." Tom said. "Imagine if you had gotten married and there had been kids."

"But I still love him."
"That will pass when you realize how much he used you . . . . Then you'll be angry."

"I could *never* be angry with Chip."

"You will be . . . . It's the only way you can get rid of this and start over."

"I don't *want* to start over."

"You will . . . . You'll have a fine life . . . . Some lucky guy will come along. . . . They'll be banging your door down."

As they worked, Tom remembered the time he and his first wife, Frances, had dinner here with Jo and Chip. After coffee, they toured photos of the young man's sailboats and viewed a display of his squash racquets.

Then they went downstairs to leave. At the curb, Frances lifted a suitcase from the back seat and handed it to Jo. They all said cheery goodbyes and Frances and Tom drove off.

He said nothing for a while, then asked:

"What's with the suitcase?"

"It was some things for Jo."

"A whole suitcase full?"

"They're living together. . . . Didn't you know that?"

"No, I didn't know that."

Frances turned into the Midtown Tunnel to Queens.

"If I had known, I wouldn't have come," Tom said.

Now, suddenly, amid the boxes and cartons, Tom
stood up straight and grim.

"Come on," he said. "Let's get the hell out of here. . . .
Leave the rest of this crap . . . . You don't need it. It's all
bad memories . . . . Let's go . . . . Your new life starts right
now."

*

COMPANIONS OF THE ROAD

Tom waved goodbye to the lumberjacks and started hiking down the trails of Mount Sunapee. It was a tough descent and when he got to the highway he was tired and wanted a lift.

He came to a stone bridge crossing a river and railroad tracks. The moon was in the river. On the bridge he tried two more sets of lights. The second car's rear lights blinked red as it pulled to the road edge beyond the bridge. Tom ran to catch it.

The driver was a stocky woman, gray haired with glasses.

"Going as far as Windsor?" Tom said. He got in. It was warm in the car.

"I don't usually pick up anyone," the woman said, eyes on the yellow center line that wove along the hill roads. "But I was kind of lonesome," she said laughing, a little embarrassed. " I'm coming from my sister's in Kingston. Drove down this morning....I had a day off....Things are a little slow at the shop."

A gleaming brace of lights topped a hill and bore down on them. She flicked her brights on and the other driver dropped his abashedly.

"My sister's taking care of her husband's folks. They're both in their 70s....You can't leave them alone any more like that....One of them might fall and the other couldn't do much."

A big galleon of the roads passed, an overnight trailer, its dark-tarpaulined bow ablaze with lights. Whoom, it said.

They passed farmhouses with warm orange windows. Jars of preserves in the windows. Families, Tom thought.

"My sister's husband is soil conservation agent over there," the woman said. "He's a good man."

Tom mentioned Stan Colby, a name he had heard from Eric.

"Yes, he's the county agent here....Who's the conservation man in Windsor now?.... I used to know his name."

"Albion Weeks."

"I knew the man before him....I've gotten a little out of touch, I guess....Well, you do.... I've been a widow for eight years now....My Ed used to know everybody...talked about them all the time."

The moon dropped behind the forest.

"I've never remarried.... Oh, I've had chances.... But

there'll never be anyone for me but my Ed…. I'm a one-man woman, I guess….Ah, well…."

They crossed the river bridge to Windsor.

"Work's been slow at the shop….They're talking about a layoff….But I'll survive…. I always have!" she added, laughing.

The car was on the smooth tarred stretch of Washington Street, passing the darkened drive-in theater and the shuttered ice cream stand.

"It's been nice having company," she said. "Country roads get lonesome."

She turned right from Washington Street and stopped at the small park with the cannon.

"Well, I go down North Street from here," she said."Thanks again."

Tom got out.

"See you again sometime," she said.

*

GRADUATION DAY

It was a lovely evening. A predicted rainstorm was holding off, and the sky beyond the ivy-hung clocktower was a soft distant blue. Tom took a seat next to Frances and watched people arriving, filling the rows of pale wooden chairs on the school lawn. There were smiling parents of all sizes and shapes, florid uncles in a seersucker jackets, aunts with blue hair, crewcut brothers home from college, fidgety little girls in pretty hats and dresses.

A green grandstand stood empty before the venerable school, waiting for the graduates-to-be, some of whom appeared fleetingly in arched doorways, wearing long blue and white robes. Tom looked for Jo. A faroff roll of thunder sounded, like the guns of an advancing army. Would it rain? As if the thunder were a cue, the orchestra arrived, boys in formal white jackets, girls in fluttering skirts, violin bows slanting like masts against a wind. A stout boy carried a gleaming shadow-whorled tuba.

Shh. Shh. They're coming.

The leader raised his baton. The music began. The graduating children came slowly down a staircase, swaying in their robes in time to the music, turning and climbing into the stands, boys in blue, girls in white. Tom saw Jo and noticed in the corner of his eye Frances taking a sip from a tiny flask.

He looked at the mass of young people, in their robes all alike.

Who were the soft-eyed scholars, who were the brawlers quick to fight, who were the drinkers headed for trouble? Who were the sweet girls made for happiness from birth, who were the wild, undisciplined girls destined for pain? Who would succeed, who would fail? Who would live long, who would not last out college and die in their glory and never be old? No telling now, in their long robes, their long flowing robes.

After the ceremonies and an exhortatory speech by a famous man, the newly anointed graduates streamed down to meet their families, and there was much laughing, and a good deal of weeping. Most of them would never see each other again.

Then they all pressed to the closed doors of the gymnasium for the annual surprise. How would it be decorated this year? Every year was different.

Then the doors were flung open, and a great sigh went up as the crowd – all children now – looked in on a scene of splendor – sultans' tents, burnished lamps, golden camels, silver fountains, a jeweled palace and overhead the storied stars of the East.

*

MATINEE

It began with Martinis at lunch. Tom Cavanaugh felt his life falling apart again. Another reporter, John Herndon, eyed him nervously as he ordered a third. Then Tom called the office and took the afternoon off, although he had been assigned to an important City Hall press conference. He pleaded a headache. City editor Johnny Potter did not seem overly sympathetic.

Herndon went back to work and Tom moved to the bar and watched the lunch crowd clear out. He liked empty bars in the afternoon. They were private and quiet. The bartender was reading a newspaper at the other end. Feeling luxuriously idle, Tom looked out the window and watched the girls go by, bosoms and bottoms swinging. Workmen were delving in a brown wound in the asphalt. A young woman walked by with two children. They were all laughing and the children clung to her skirt, looking up adoringly. Does she know this is the happiest time of her life? Tom wondered. Well, maybe it is and maybe . . . .
"Go get 'em, kids," he said aloud anyhow, and the bartender looked up, frowning. Tom asked for a cognac.

When he got outside, the sun hurt his eyes. He was feeling reckless. He took a cab to a place Herndon had told him about. Even remembered the address. Felt pretty good about that.

A dark, hard-looking man let him in when he mentioned Herndon's name. He has contempt for me, Tom thought. Can see it in his eyes. Having to pay for it. *Hey, Goombah!* he thought, but prudently did not say. Mob controls all these dumps. Could get nasty. Be great for my brilliant career if there's a Goddamned raid.

A handsome black woman in a green satin dress met him and led him to a room full of girls in bikinis. This is wonderful, Tom thought happily. Like a buffet. Everything looks so good. The girls watched him expectantly. One winked and licked her lips. Tom picked a caramel-colored girl in two tiny strips of white silk and followed her down a corridor. Walking behind her, he was full of admiration. She was beautiful. Right off a Caribbean travel poster. The wonders of the islands. Bikinis and high heels go so well together.

They went into a small room. Sparsely furnished, with bed and sofa, a table with glasses. When Tom said he wanted to stay for the afternoon, the girl had to discuss it with management.

He asked her to bring back some Scotch. She returned in a little while and said it was all right. They sat on the little sofa and had their drinks, the girl just sipping, faking it really.
He looked at her sitting next to him. So beautiful. It was all such a simple arrangement. He took her hand and kissed her lightly on her shining cheekbone. She raised her mouth and he kissed her long and deeply. I must be crazy, he thought. She stroked him and began undoing his trousers. He undid her bra and took it off, gauzy little thing to hold such riches. Her breasts were even fuller than they had looked. Dark purple nipples. Winedark. He kissed them, then put his mouth on them. Her hand worked softly. He sat back, and she leaned over.

When he awoke alone a few hours later in the desolate, sour-smelling room, it was blue twilight. Birds were squeaking at the window

.

*

A HANDFUL OF DUST

Having Danny home is a strain, Frances Cavanaugh thought. He's so gaunt, thinner than ever -- the way his father was after our own breakup. "You always pay for the things you do," I told him when I was leaving with the kids. He cried like a baby. I had the power then. Let him suffer, as I had. As Danny is suffering now, and me too really, with the loneliness.

Danny's never been able to forgive him. When we came back here after the break, I'd see the little guy standing on the sofa, looking out the window. I finally asked him what he was doing. "I'm waiting for Daddy to come in the car and take us back to Vermont," he said. The day I told him we were not going back to Vermont, his face went dead.

The child is a darling though. So talkative. Does she realize yet what's happened to her little life? These things start out so happily. Maybe they're not even supposed to last. Are we just like the other creatures, coming tougher for warmth, young ones, then drifting apart? Sex gives us the greatest joys and the greatest sorrows of our lives. Better to have done it though. Otherwise an empty life.

"Where is that girl anyhow?" Frances said aloud. She put down her coffee and newspaper, went to the screen door and looked out at the summer morning.

She's restless with her father in the city job-hunting -- and looking the way he does. Those two are close -- maybe too close. I'm restless too. Slept badly again. Probably the heat -- and all this emotional nonsense -- going through it again at my age. I thought it was over and done with.

In her bare feet, she went along the gravel driveway toward the road, wanting her coffee and another cigarette. She stopped to admire the new paint on the Wyleys' house. Deep burgundy and white shutters. Pretty.

She called the child's name aloud.

"I'm in Mrs. Wyley's garden, Grandma,'" Deirdre answered. "Come help me. I'm picking flowers for Mommy's birthday. Mrs. Wyley said I could."

She stood in the garden, her arms full, hair wet. A tousled nymph in a silk nightgown. The hyacinth girl.

"That's nice, but not too many now."

"Help me. There are some I can't reach."

Frances went into the garden, reeling at its colors and scents. The fragrant grass was dewy and her feet were suddenly wet and cool. It was like the garden she tended so carefully the year Tom was overseas.

She forgot her coffee, her cigarettes, the papers, who's in, who's out, great ones that ebb and flow by the moon. Grandmother and child cut flowers in a morning garden with shimmering butterflies and black- and gold-vested bees their only courtiers.

This is so lovely, Frances thought, her arms abrim with pink, white and yellow blossoms. reciting their names, and the names of the birds too, there on the garage roof. Like the doves on our porch in Vermont. And Rod Morton's barn swallows at the lake. The things you remember.

"Your mother will love these, Deirdre . . . . Wrap them in the silver paper I have."

Blossom-laden, they clipped and sorted in the scented alcove.

Then, inevitably, reality broke in, with things to do, calls to make.

"I think that's enough, Deirdre . . . . Mrs. Wyley has been very nice."

"Grandma, *stay*."

"You have enough now . . . . and I have to give Schatzie his breakfast."

"Oh, *Grandma*!"

Frances made her way across the grass toward the driveway. The gravel hurt her feet.

"Grandma, *come back!*"

Frances stopped and looked at the child.

Should I return? Could it continue?

But the light is changing. The sun is drying the dew.

Too late!

*

www.ingramcontent.com/pod-product-compliance
Lightning Source LLC
Chambersburg PA
CBHW071630140626
46555CB00021B/1941